The Peopling of Australia

Introduction

Until recent times the Aboriginal people lived as a Stone Age civilization. Though technologically primitive, their society produced a culture both rich in mythological lore and vast in its knowledge of the natural world. Amazingly they have passed this great body of information from generation to generation without the assistance of the written word. Instead, they have relied upon their oral tradition.

Archaeologists are beginning to prove the validity of some of the Aboriginal claims based on the age-old oral tradition. For example, the Aboriginals claim they arrived in Australia from a land to the northwest. Archaeologists agree that indeed these people did arrive from lands northwest of Australia, probably India or Southeastern Asia via Indonesia and the Melanesian islands thousands of years ago. The Peopling of Australia is a brief history which incorporates both the Aboriginal and modern archaeologists' and paleontologists' view of Australia's ancient history.

Author Percy Trezise grew up in the Australian bush which fostered his love of nature. In 1960 he met the aspiring Aboriginal artist, Dick Roughsey, whose Aboriginal name was Goobalathaldin. Together they began a partnership in painting, writing, and exploring, which endured 25 years until Roughsey's death. Trezise continues to document the legends and lore of the Aboriginal people through his painting and writing. In 1983, he received the Advance Australia award for his outstanding contributions to Australian art and culture.

Library of Congress Cataloging-in-Publication Data

Trezise, Percy.
  The peopling of Australia.

  (Stories of the dreamtime — tales of the Aboriginal people)
  Summary: Describes the very early days of Australia, when its
first people shared the land with dangerous beasts and began to
develop their culture and traditions.
  1. Australian aborigines—Juvenile literature. [1. Australian aborigines]
I. Trezise, Percy, ill. II. Title. III. Series: Stories of the dreamtime.
GN666.T72   1987   994'.0049915   88-20124
ISBN 1-55532-950-0 (lib. bdg.)

North American edition first published in 1988 by

Gareth Stevens, Inc.
7317 West Green Tree Road
Milwaukee, WI 53223 USA

First published in Australia by William Collins Pty. Ltd.

Editor: Kathy Keller
Introduction: Kathy Keller
Map: Mario Macari
Design: Kate Kriege

1 2 3 4 5 6 7 8 9 92 91 90 89 88

The Peopling of Australia

story and art by

PERCY TREZISE

Gareth Stevens Publishing
Milwaukee

Many millions of years ago Australia was part of a supercontinent, Gondwanaland. It was a reptilian world where huge dinosaurs fed upon the tops of palms, and giant allosaurs ate the smaller dinosaurs and other reptiles.

4

Long after the dinosaurs died out, Australia broke away from the other continents and drifted northward. It was like a giant life raft carrying all the developing species of marsupials and other animals which became unique to Australia.

5

By the late Ice Age, 200,000 years ago, Australia was a rich and verdant land teeming with all kinds of animals and birds. There were giant kangaroos and emus and many species of gentle giants called diprotodons.

Great forests covered much of the continent, and there were large rivers, lakes and swamps. There was no one to utilize the riches because it was still a land awaiting its people.

The first Australians came more than 100,000 years ago and probably arrived by raft via Java. They were surely the world's most fortunate people, for they entered a beautiful land which was like the Garden of Eden.

The giant birds and animals, innocent of the ways of human hunters, were easy to capture. There was an abundance of fruit and other plant foods. No wonder they were a happy people.

As the small band of first settlers grew in numbers, they spread across the land in family groups. They named and hunted all the animals, big and small. They called the gentle diprotodons *kadimakara*, and the big emus *mihirung*.

They discovered there was danger in the land. Huge crocodiles lived in most of the rivers, and marsupial lions roamed the forests. Perhaps the most dangerous animal of all was a giant goanna, called *megalania*.

There was also danger from active volcanoes and earthquakes. Aboriginal mythology still recalls that the mountains exploded and the ground opened up and swallowed people.

There were fearful times when all the land trembled, the air was full of smoke and ash, and the sky was a red never seen before.

Sometimes the hunters became the hunted. If not careful, a hunter could be pounced on by a megalania lurking among the bushes. Along the rivers, there were giant snakes ever ready to grab the unwary animal, or human, for lunch.

However, like people everywhere, they soon learned what dangers their world held and how to avoid them. With sharp wits, clubs, and spears, they were able to defend themselves and their children.

In many parts of Australia, the early people found ready-made homes in which they could find shelter from storms and rain. These were caves in the base of a sandstone cliff, some large enough to hold hundreds of people.

When the nights were cold, sheets of soft paper bark, from trees along the river, served as mattresses and blankets. In those early times, people everywhere lived in caves and rock shelters.

Eventually the people covered the entire continent and the island of Tasmania. Everywhere they found plenty of kadimakara, kangaroos, and emus, as well as plant foods.

The travels of the first ancestors and the things they found in their new land are still remembered in tribal lore. They recognized the spirits of the land and its natural laws and passed this knowledge on to their children.

In the southlands, the weather was much colder, with snow and
ice on the mountains. There were few caves, so the people built
their own winter shelters of stone and bark. They made warm fur
cloaks from possum and kangaroo skins.

To make hunting easier, they built large fish traps of stone, and made string to fashion nets for fowl and fish. They made stone axes to cut honey from hollow trees, and invented the wommera to help throw spears further.

About 20,000 years ago, the waning Ice Age ended the good life. Fierce droughts parched the land, and the rivers, lakes, and swamps dried up. The poor kadimakara and other large animals were too big and slow to travel long distances between food and water. They died and became extinct.

Many people suffered and died. Laws were made to protect the remaining animals and other foods. The main law said: *No one must ever kill an animal made poor by drought. In drought all must become poor, including humans, so that all may survive the hard times.*

When the ice caps melted, the seas rose and covered much of the coastal land, displacing many clans. Many swamplands rich in food were lost when the sea flooded in, forming places like the Gulf of Carpentaria.

Only the hardiest and wisest people survived the great changes and learned to live harmoniously with Nature. The women and children gathered the small game and plant foods with care. The men burned patches of grass so there were green shoots for the kangaroos to eat.

The people's religion sprang from the Dreamtime, in the time of creation. In the Dreamtime, all living things on Earth had human shape. Floods, volcanoes, ice, and fires frightened many of the people so terribly that they changed into plants, birds, animals, and insects for refuge.

The remaining people had to take responsibility for their changed relatives and developed art forms to express their reverence for them. Rock paintings, with their stories and ceremonies, were handed down from generation to generation, so that none should ever forget.

Eventually trade routes criss-crossed the entire continent. Along these routes, the people exchanged tools, weapons, ceremonial objects, songs, and ceremonies. They knew of each other from north to south and east to west.

28

Clans often traveled vast distances to gather together for marriage ceremonies and the secret, sacred initiation ceremonies where young men learned of the heroic deeds of their ancestors, and of the secrets of life beyond the grave.

Then, one morning about 200 years ago, some of the Eora clan watched in astonishment as eleven sailing ships dropped anchor in a bay on the southeast coast of Australia. Their long, long epoch of Aboriginal history was about to end.

Aboriginal civilization, which revered the land and its spiritual values, was conquered and deprived of its clan lands by a civilization based on material values. Today most Aboriginals live on reservations. They still mourn the loss of their homelands and ancient ways.

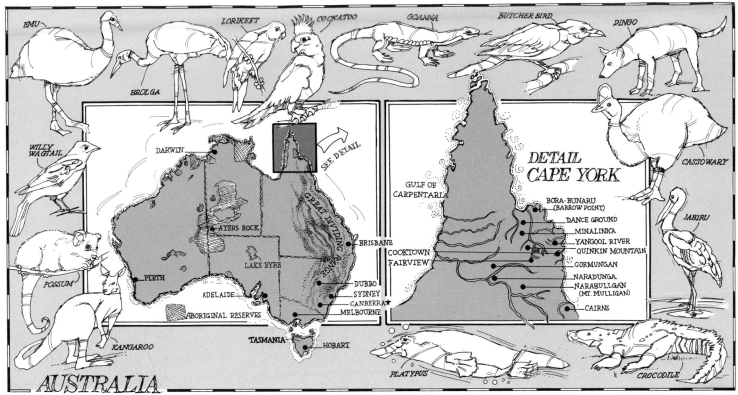

AUSTRALIA

Glossary

clan: a group of families claiming a common ancestor

diprotodon (di PRO toe don): a very large, now extinct marsupial

Dreamtime: the time long ago in Aboriginal mythology when supernatural ancestors created the world

emu (E myu): a three-toed flightless bird related to the ostrich

epoch: a period of history which is considered remarkable, or marked by distinct events

extinct: dead and gone, with no other member of the same species left alive

goanna (go AHN nah): an Australian lizard

Gondwanaland (gahn DWAHN ah land): one of two supercontinents

ice caps: a cap of ice over an area sloping down from the middle on all sides

initiation: a ceremony which allows new members to join a group or society

kadimakara (kah dee mah KAH rah): a giant marsupial, now extinct

marsupials (mar SU pee ulls): any of the various mammals such as the kangaroo, which nurse and carry their young in a skin pouch on their abdomen

megalania (meg ah LAHN ee ah): an extinct, giant lizard which died out 20,000 years ago

mihirung (mih HE rung): an extinct, giant emu

mythology: a collection of myths, or stories, of supernatural beings and events

reptilian: reptile-like

species: a group of animals having some common characteristics

supercontinent: one of two huge continents (Gondwanaland and Laursia) that made up all the land on Earth about 150 million years ago

Tasmania (taz MAYN ee ah): an island off the southeastern coast of Australia, one of the six states of the Commonwealth of Australia

verdant: covered with living plants or grasses

wommera (WOMM er ah): a stick or sling used by the Aboriginals to throw darts or spears

32